엘리트 시선 47

꽃과 바람과 詩

장 현 경 시집

엘리트출판사

꽃과 바람과 詩

장 현 경 시집

엘리트출판사

아름다운 꽃들의 이야기 4

봄이 오면, 한강 하류에 군락을 이룬 실버들이 하늘하늘 휘늘어져 상춘객을 부르고 강변에 피어 있는 철쭉꽃의 그윽한 향기를 맡으며 아름다운 꽃들의 이야기를 그려 본다. 꽃들도 인간처럼 각기 그 특성이 있다고 하겠다. 시기 질투의 대명사라면 단연 담배꽃이 아닐 수 없다. 세계에서 가장 못생긴 꽃은 라플레시아꽃이다. 꽃나무에 심취할수록 불로장생을 돕고 재앙을 막아주는 감국꽃. 돈을 잘 벌게 해주는 천양금꽃. 용감한 병사로 알려진 투구꽃. 사약(死藥)의 선수는 흰독말풀꽃. 육식하는 파리지옥꽃. 전쟁광 시스투스꽃은 주변의 경쟁자를 모조리 무찌르기 위해 스스로 부름켜에서 휘발성 오일을 분비하여 온 산야를 불태워버린다. 시스투스 자신은 불에 잘 견디는 씨앗으로 잿더미에서 다시 싹을 틔워 대를 이어간다.

인간이 대지 위에 몸을 맡기고 살아가듯이, 사람은 자연과 공존하는 존재다. 꽃나무에서 공기를 얻고, 물로 인간의 몸을 구성하기에 인간은 자연에 종속되고 의존해야만 하는 존재다. 생태계에서 중요한 것은 적대와 갈등이 아니라 협력과 상호의존이다. 인간

존재의 근원이 있게 하는 자연 즉 꽃의 중요성과 그 의미에 천착하는 것은 언어를 조탁하는 시인들의 임무일 것이다. 이런 점에서 인간이 자연의 순환성을 거스르지 않고 사는 방법에 대해 시인은 자신의 시를 통해 설명하고 있다.

꽃을 보니 눈이 시원해지고 마음도 밝아지고 기분마저 좋아진다. 시인으로 움츠린 몸에 기지개를 켜며 사계절 지지 않는 꽃들의 이야기를 소재로 여기 한 권의 영역 시집을 다듬는다. 꽃들의 이야기가 이 어려운 시대를 견뎌내는 수많은 독자에게 위로와 희망, 감동이 되기를 기대합니다.

늘 따뜻한 성원을 보내주신 가족과 이웃의 지지에 고마운 마음 전하며 청계문학 가족 여러분의 건승을 빕니다. 나의 시편들을 만나는 존경하는 독자님께 건강과 행복이 늘 함께하시기를 기원합니다.

2022년 1월 청계서재(淸溪書齋)에서
자정(紫井) 장현경(張鉉景) 근정(謹呈)

The Story of Beautiful Flowers 4

When spring comes, silvers that form a colony in the lower reaches of the Han River flutter in the sky and invite visitors to come, and draw the story of beautiful flower while smelling the sweet scent of azaleas blooming along the riverbank. Flowers, like humans, have their own characteristics. If it is a symbol of envy and jealousy, it is by no means a tobacco flower. The ugliest flower in the world is the rafflesia. The chrysanthemum flower that helps immortality and prevents disasters the more you fall in love with the flowering tree. Thousand gold flower that makes money well. helmed flower known as a brave soldier. The player of venenosity is white poison ivy flower. A carnivorous fly-hell flower. In order to defeat all nearby competitors, the war-crazy Cistus flower calls itself and releases volatile oil from it, burning the entire mountain field. Cistus himself is a fire-tolerant seed that will sprout again from the ashes and pass on through generations.

Just as humans entrust their bodies to the earth and live,

humans coexist with nature. To obtain air from flowering trees and to compose the human body with water, humans are subordinate and dependent on nature. What is important in an ecosystem is cooperation and interdependence, not antagonism and conflict. It would be the poet's job to craft a language to delve into the importance and meaning of nature, that is, the source of human existence. In this regard, the poet is explaining through his poems how humans live without going against the cycle of nature.

Seeing flowers refreshes my eyes, brightens my heart, and improves my mood. I stretch my body as a poet and refine a book of poems translated into English here with the story of flowers that do not fade in the four seasons. It is hoped that the story of flowers will provide comfort, hope, and inspiration to many readers who are enduring these difficult times.

I would like to express my gratitude to the support of my family and neighbors who have always given me warm support, and I wish the Cheonggye Literature family all the best. To my dear readers who meet my psalms, I wish you good health and good fortune.

January 2022 in Cheonggye Library

Jajeong, Jang Hyunkyung Raising

물매화꽃

높은 산 바위틈에
물매화가 화사하게 피어 있다

어린 시절
이 먼 곳에
놀았던 그 흔적
늘 그리워했는데

세월이 흘러
이곳에 올 줄
어떻게 알았을까

기다리고 있었다는 듯
고결한 물매화

송이송이 피어
미소짓고 있네!

Water Plum Blossom

In the high mountain rocks
The water plum blossoms brightly

Childhood
In the distance
The trace of playing
I've always missed you

Years pass
Will come here
How did you know?

As if waiting
Noble water plum

Per the blossom
You're smiling!

contents

제1부 알리섬꽃

제2부 무릇꽃

제3부 부용화

제4부 아로니아꽃 그대

제5부 포인세티아꽃

제1부

알리섬꽃

그렇게 살 거라고
오늘도 내일도
피고 지고.

튤립꽃

종 모양의 꽃이
강한 느낌을 주면서
아름다움을 지니고 있어

사랑을 고백하려는 이에게
주고 싶은 빨간색 튤립

영원한 사랑을 꿈꾸는 이에게
주고 싶은 보라색 튤립

격려하며 사랑하는 이에게
주고 싶은 분홍색 튤립

커플들이 서로 선물하기에
좋은 망고 색 튤립

화해하고
용서해주고 싶은 커플들이
서로 찾는 하얀색 튤립

싫어한다는 의사 표시를
하고 싶을 때는 검은색 튤립

이루어질 수 없는 사랑을
고백하고 싶을 때는
노란색 튤립

안개꽃과 잘 어울려
선물할 때
매력 쨍 쨍!

Tulip Flower

Bell-shaped flowers
Giving you a strong feeling
Have beauty

To those who want to confess their love
I want to give you a red tulip

To those who dream of eternal love
I want to give you purple tulips

Encourage and love
Pink tulips to give

For couples to gift each other
Nice mango color tulips

Reconcile
Couples who want to forgive
White tulips looking for each other

Express dislike
Black tulips when you want

An impossible love
When you want to confess
Yellow tulips

Goes well with the mist flower
When gifting
Charm dazzling!

앵두나무꽃

봄에 보는 앵두나무
수줍음이 가득

봄소식을 전하려
잎은 나중에
꽃부터 먼저 피우네

해마다 볼수록
더 반가운 앵두나무

오직 한 사람을 사랑하는 앵두나무꽃
활짝 피어
꾀꼬리 소리 들리고

봄바람에
꽃비가 내리고

코로나19도
꽃비와 같이
우수수 떨어져 사라지기를

앵두는 염원한다.

Downy Cherry Blossom

Cherry tree in spring
Full of shyness

I'm going to tell you about spring
The leaves later
Flowers bloom first

The more you see each year
A more welcome cherry

A cherry flower that loves only one person
In full bloom
I can hear a whistle

In the spring breeze
With the rain of flowers

Corona 19 degrees
Like a rain of flowers
Let the rain fall and disappear

The cherry desires.

꽃기린꽃

어느 추운 겨울날

오랜만에
친구 집에 갔는데

그 집에 들어서자마자
가장 눈에 띄는 것이
베란다 화초

가까이 보니
가시 돋친 줄기에
작고 빨간 꽃이
앙증맞게 피어

꽃기린을 배경으로
사진 한 장 찰칵!

나올 때
화분 하나를 받아 와
책상 위에 놓고

가시 면류관을 쓰고
고난의 깊이를 간직한
예수님의 꽃을
기쁜 마음으로 그리며

밤에 산소를 내뿜는
꽃기린꽃과
밤을 지새운다.

Flower Giraffe Flower

A cold winter day

After a long time
I went to my friend's house

As soon as I entered the house
The most striking thing
Veranda flowering plant

I can see close
On the thorny stem
A small red flower
A small bloom

In the background of the flower giraffe
One click of a picture!

When it comes out
Get me a pot
On the desk

With a visible cotton tube
With the depth of hardship
Jesus flower
Missing with joy

It gives off oxygen at night
With a flower giraffe
I spend the night.

비올라꽃

겨울에도 꽃을 피우며
시원한 날씨를 좋아하는
비올라꽃은
추위에 강하고

색깔이
만물이 소생하는 봄과
잘 어울린다

키가 작아
땅을 덮으며 자라는 비올라꽃

관광객을 맞으며
항상 따뜻한 마음을
전해주고

철 따라
그대와 사랑을
그리워하며

꽃 가꾸기를 취미로
삶의 아름다움을
수놓네!

Viola Flower

In winter, flowering
A cool weather-loving
Viola flower
Strong against the cold

Color
With spring where everything comes
You looked great

Be short
A viola flower growing over the ground

In the face of tourists
Always warm heart
To tell him

Seasonally
Love with you
In longing

As a hobby to grow flowers
The beauty of life
Embroidery!

알리섬꽃

귀여운 알리섬꽃
옹기종기 군락을 지어
여기저기
피고 지고

봄가을
탓하지 않고
또 만나
피고 지고

지금보다 더
우아함을 자극하여
빼어난 미모로
기품 있는 인상을 주려고

달콤한 향기로
뛰어난 아름다움을 보여주려고

그렇게 살 거라고
오늘도 내일도
피고 지고.

Alisum Flower

Cute alisum flower
Form a swarm
Here and there
Suffer and lose

Spring fall
Without blaming
See you again
Suffer and lose

More than now
To stimulate elegance
With great beauty
To give a dignified impression

With a sweet scent
To show off her outstanding beauty

I'll live like that
Today and tomorrow
Defend and lose.

자귀나무꽃

해가 질 무렵에
활짝 피는 꽃

낮에는 펼치고
밤에는 붙는 잎사귀

나무 모양이 풍성하여
향긋한 꽃향기가
머리를 맑게 하고

가슴 두근거림을
치료해주는 수피(樹皮)

꽃송이 모양이
공작새 깃털 같아

부부 금실의 상징
환희의 자귀나무꽃!

Silk Tree Flower

At sunset
Blooming flowers

Spread out during the day
Leaves that stick at night

The shape of the tree is rich
Fragrant floral scent
Clear your head

Chest palpitations
Healing tree bark

Flower shape
Like a peacock feather

Symbol of couple gold thread
The silk tree blossoms of joy!

라플레시아꽃

이파리와 줄기가 없어
열대 정글을
기어 다니며

알같이 생긴 꽃봉오리가
여기저기 솟아나
신기하고 두렵다

활짝 핀 꽃송이
썩은 고기 같아
무섭게 보이고

기생하고 살면서
이리 큰 꽃을 피워

꽃 같지 않은 꽃
볼수록 신기하여
장대한 미를 느끼게 하네!

Rafflesia Flower

No leaves and no stems
Tropical jungle
Crawling

Egg-shaped flower buds
Springing up here and there
Strange and scary

Flower in full bloom
Like rotten meat
Looks scary

Live and live
Make a big flower

Flower that are not like flowers
The more I see, the more interesting
It makes me feel grandiose!

시클라멘꽃

식물원에 들어서니
곱게 핀 시클라멘꽃에
마음과 시선이 간다

두 팔 들고
만세 부르는 듯
새가 훨훨 나는 듯
나비가 나풀나풀 내려앉는 듯

초겨울부터 화려하게 피어
겨우내
예쁜 모습을 보여준다

꽃대에서 핀 꽃이
왕관이 되듯

수줍은 마음이
때로는 시기 질투심으로
나타나기도

여름에 잠자고
가을에 깨어나
시클라멘꽃이 가장 살기 좋은 곳

햇빛이 잘 드는 베란다.

Cyclamen Flower

I'm in a botanical garden
In the finely-finished cyclamen flower
I have a heart and a gaze

With both arms up
Like a long call
Like a bird is flying
As if the butterfly were falling

Blooming brilliantly from early winter
Throughout the winter
Show a pretty look

The flowers in the flower bed
As a crown

A shy mind
Sometimes with jealousy
Manifestation

Sleeping in the summer

Wake up in the fall

The best place for cyclamen flowers to live

A sunny veranda.

노블 칼랑코에꽃

봄 봄
봄이 왔네

베란다 정원에서
빨갛게
피고 있는 노블 칼랑코에꽃에
설렘의 키스를 하고

자잘하고
동글동글한 꽃이
다발로 모여 있어
집안이 환하네

가까이 보니
작은 꽃에 비해
유난히 크고 두꺼운 잎
메말라 시드는 일은 없겠네

일 년 내내 꽃을 피워
오밀조밀
참으로 예쁘다.

Noble Kalanchoe Flower

Spring spring
Spring has come

In the veranda garden
Red
The blooming noble kalanchoe flower
With a thrilling kiss

In small hands
A dongle-down flower
They're clustered together
The house is bright

I can see close
In comparison to the small flowers
Exceptionally large and thick leaf
I'm sure you're not going to get sick

They bloom all year round
Dense
She's so beautiful.

무스카리꽃

햇빛이 드는 베란다 정원

가을에 심은
무스카리 구근이 싹을 틔워

꽃대가 살그머니 올라와
종 모양처럼 생긴
작은 꽃봉오리들이 빽빽하게
무리 지어 핀다

세월이 흘러
눈이 내리고

올망졸망 매달린
청자색 무스카리 열매

색상도 신비로워
멀리서 보면
맛있는 포도송이

다시 보면
그림의 떡!

Muscari Flower

A sunny veranda garden

Autumn-planted
Muscari bulb sprout

The flowerbeds are creeping up
Bell-like
The small buds are densely packed
Pack up

As time goes by
With snow

Clung to the top
Blue-colored muscari fruit

The color is mysterious
From a distance
Delicious grapes

I'll look back
Pie in the sky.

꽃과 바람과 詩

제2부

무릇꽃

짝사랑처럼
잎과 꽃이 서로
만나지 못해
그리움을 담고 있네!

때죽나무꽃

사람들이
오가는 산책로에

때가 많아
검게 보이는 줄기에
조롱조롱
매달린 때죽나무꽃

때로는 열매 찧은 물로
물고기를 떼로 잡고
빨래하여 때를 뺀다

꽃송이가 달린 모양
하얗게 수줍은 듯
겸손해 보이고

향기를 흩날리며
멀리서도 울리는 종소리에
지나는 이의 발길을
멈추게 한다.

Styrax Japonica Flower

People
On the walkway

There are many dirts
Black-looking stem
Like a gaggle
Dangling styrax japonica flower

Sometimes it's a fruity water
I'm gonna grab a bunch of fish
Wash out dirts

A flowered shape
White and shy
Looking humble

Flaming with scent
The sound of a bell ringing from a distance
The passerby's footsteps
It stops.

동자꽃

등산객이 좋아하는 동자꽃
인기 좋고
흔하게 피는
산간지역 야생화

한여름
높은 산 암자에서
스님을 기다리는 듯
활짝 피어 있네

주황색 동자꽃(童子花)
바람에 팔랑거리며

밤하늘의 별과 함께
사랑 노래 부르며
산이 좋아
산에서 사노라네!

Lychnis Flower

A favorite lychnis flower for hikers
Popular
Common blood
Wild flowers in mountainous areas

Midsummer
In the high mountain hermitage
As if waiting for the monk
It's blooming

Orange child flower
With the wind

With the stars in the night sky
Singing love songs
I like mountains
Live in the mountains.

동의나불꽃

둥근 잎을 깔때기 모양으로 말아
물을 떠서
목을 축일 수 있는 작은 동이

기분을 밝고 산뜻하게
해주는 샛노란 꽃

예쁜 잎사귀
쭉쭉 뻗은 줄기에서
보여주는 다양한 조형미에서

자신이 꽃이 되는 듯
다가올 행복을 느낀다.

Kingcup Flower

Roll round leaves into funnel shapes
With water
A small jar that can moisten the neck

Brightly and freshly
A bright yellow flower

A pretty leaf
In the stretch of stem
In the various formative beauty shown

As if you were a flower
I feel happiness coming.

연영초꽃

석 장의 푸근한 이파리
그 위에
석 장의 꽃받침
그 위에
석 장의 꽃잎이 피는
순백의 아름다운 꽃을

그윽한 마음으로
바라보는 사람들

열매와 뿌리
한약재로 쓰일 때
수명이 연장되어
돋보이는 풀

한 번 볼 때마다
한 살씩 젊어진다는
연영초(延齡草)꽃.

Trillium Flower

Three warm leaves
On top of it
Three calyx
On top of it
Three petal-floating
Beautiful pure white flowers

With a hearty heart
The people who look at

Fruit and root
It is used as the material of herbal medicine
With an extended life span
A striking grass

Every time I look at it
Getting younger one year at a time.
Trillium flower.

두루미꽃

두루미의 고고한 자태로
우아하게 느껴지는 야생화

초여름
촘촘하게 군락을 이루어
예쁘게 피어 있네

두루미의 목을 닮은
이삭 모양의 꽃차례로

화려하게
날개를 펼쳐
기어가는 듯한 이파리

가는 줄기
두툼한 이파리가
작은 꽃과 무리 지어
날아다니는 두루미 떼.

Crane Flower

In the noble form of a crane
A wild flower that feels elegant

Early summer
Densely, community is accomplished
It's blooming pretty

A crane-like neck
A panicle in the shape of grain

Glamorously
Spread the wing
A crawling leaf

Thin stem
A thick leaf
In small groups of flowers
A bunch of flying cranes.

비비추꽃

연한 잎을 나물로 이용할 때
거품이 나올 때까지
손으로 비벼
비비추꽃

하늘이 내린 인연으로
신비로운 사람이
나타나

인연을 맺어주는
기쁜 소식

한여름 비비추꽃
무리 지어

화관은 종 모양으로
연분홍 자주색으로 피어

당당하게
계절을 알린다.

Hosta Flower

The light leaf is used as the herbs
Until the bubbles come out
Rub it with your hands
Hosta flower

With a relationship of heaven
A mysterious man
Show up

A connection
Good news

Midsummer hosta flower
In a group

In the form of a bell
Pink purple

With pride
Informing the season.

오동나무꽃

오동나무는 가볍고 연하다

무늬가 아름답고
습기에 강하고
잘 뒤틀어지지 않아
악기를 낳는다

소리의 전달 성능도 좋아
가야금 거문고로 탄생한다

오동나무
천년이 지나도
가락을 잃지 않는다

고상한 색깔의 종처럼
생겨
한낮에도 환하게
꽃등을 켠
연보라색 오동나무꽃

딸을 낳으면
오동나무를 심어
같이 자란다.

Paulownia Flower

The paulownia is light and soft

Beautiful in pattern
Strong in moisture
It doesn't twist well
Produce musical instruments

Sound transmission performance is also good
It is born as a gayageum and geomungo

Paulownia
After a thousand years
Keep the tune

Like a noble-coloured bell
Accrue
Brightly in the middle of the day
Flower-lighted
Pale purple of paulownia flower

If you have a daughter
Plant a paulownia tree
We grow up together.

무릇꽃

여름 끝자락에 피는 무릇꽃
가을바람으로
보랏빛 꽃을 피운다

인내심이 강한 무릇꽃
자제력도 강해

허리 무릎 관절 손발이
쑤시고 아플 때
달여서 먹으면

혈액순환이 잘되어
건강에 도움이 되지만

짝사랑처럼
잎과 꽃이 서로
만나지 못해
그리움을 담고 있네!

Chinese Squill Flower

A flower blooming at the end of summer
In the autumn wind
Bloom purple flowers

A patient flower
Self-control is strong

Waist knee joints and feet
When it hurts and hurts
Sweetened

Well circulation
It's good for your health

Like unrequited love
The leaf and flower each other
I can't meet him
I'm missing you!

개별꽃

나지막한 산에서 자라
밤하늘에
별을 닮은 야생의 꽃이여!

너무 작아
군락을 이루니
볼수록 귀엽다

잎은 나물로
뿌리는 다양한 약재로
쓰이는 데다가

인삼 뿌리를 능가하는
태자삼(太子蔘) 담금주를 보고
너도나도
손이 가네!

Heterophylly Flower

Grow up in a low mountain
In the night sky
Wild flowers resembling stars!

It's too small
In the community
The more you see, the more cute you are

Leaves are herbs
Rooting is a variety of medicinal materials
Used and used

Surpassing ginseng root
Seeing the dipping sauce of the Crown Prince
You too
I'm out of hand!

잔대꽃

어느 날
아침 이슬 머금은 초롱꽃에서
아침을 깨우는 종소리
은은하게 들리네

가을빛 짙어질 때
보라색 층층 등불로
주위를 밝힌다

층층잔대 한뿌리 찾으러
나선 길

언제나 그 자리에서
은은한 향기
소박한 모습의 꽃을 보네

산야의 그늘진 모래땅에서
잘 자란 사삼(沙蔘)

약효가 인삼에 버금가고
해독작용은 물론
백 가지 독을 풀 수 있어
인간의 수명을 길게 하는
은혜의 식물.

Stalk Flower

One day
In the morning dewy lantern
A bell waking up in the morning
Hear it softly

When autumn is thick
Purple layered lantern
Light up the surroundings

To find a single root
Spiral path

Always on the spot
A subtle scent
See a simple flowers

In the shadowy sandy lands of the mountains
The well-grown ginseng

The medicinal effect is comparable to the ginseng

Detoxification

You can release a hundred poisons

Longing human life

Plants of grace.

뻐꾹나리꽃

우연히
숲속을 거닐다가
눈에 띈 뻐꾹나리꽃

나뭇가지에서 떨어지려는 이파리가
최후의 기도를 하려는 듯이

뻐꾸기 목덜미를 닮아
연한 자색의 반점이 박힌
뻐꾹나리꽃을 보고

고향 생각이 절로 나
뻐꾸기 울음소리에
고개를 갸우뚱
숲속의 적막을 흔든다

아름다운 무늬와 색상으로
꽃이 핀
그리운 고향 땅 하늘은
영원히 당신의 것.

Cuckoo Nari Flower

By chance
Walk through the woods
A conspicuous flower

The leaves that are about to fall off the branches
As if to say the last prayer

Like the neck of a cuckoo
Light purple-stained
I saw the cuckoo nari flower

I'm thinking about my hometown
The cuckoo's crying
A head cock
Shake the silence of the forest

In beautiful patterns and colors
Flowering
The skies of the land
Yours forever.

꽃과 바람과 詩

제3부

부용화

재색을 겸비한
정숙한 여인으로

금불초꽃

산들바람이
나뭇잎을 흔들고

풀잎 사이를 스쳐
나부끼는 황금빛 부처꽃

노란 꽃송이마다
향기롭고
강한 생명력이 느껴지는
부처의 숨소리

금불초꽃을 보고
상큼한 하루를
그려보네!

Elecampane Flower

A breeze
Waving leaves

Brush between the grass leaves
A bald golden Buddha

Every yellow flower bud
Fragrant
Strong-lived
The breathing of Buddha

I saw the elecampane flower
A fresh day
I'm drawing it!

뻐꾹채꽃

화사한 봄날에
뻐꾸기 우는 소리를 듣고
피는 홍자색 뻐꾹채꽃

꽃받침이
뻐꾸기의 앞가슴
깃털을 닮았네

따스한 봄철에
뻐꾹채 여린 잎을 먹고
봄의 나그네인 양

이산 저산
돌아다니는 뻐꾸기

뻐꾹 뻐꾹….

Cuckoo Flower

On a bright spring day
Hear the cuckoo crowing
Blooming red purple flower

Calyx
The front chest of a cuckoo
It looks like a feather

In the warm spring
Cuckoo eats tender leaves
Like a spring traveler

This mountain, that mountain
Wandering cuckoo

Cuckoo cuckoo···.

투구꽃

뾰족한 이파리에
꽃도 예쁜데

약재로 쓰이고
독화살을 만들고
사약의 재료로도 쓰이는 투구꽃

진보라 빛 모아
땅에 깔고

세상을 향해
부르짖는 신비한 비밀

'나를 건드리지 마!'

Helmed Flower

On a pointed leaf
Flowers are pretty, too

Used as a medicinal herb
Make a poison arrow.
A helmet flower also used as a material for the poison

Gathering the light of violet
On the ground

Towards the world
A secret of a cry

'Don't touch me!'

공작초꽃

어디에서나
항상 좋은 기분으로
살아가려고

저마다의 몸짓으로
긴 줄기에
작은 꽃들이
오밀조밀 피어

공작새가 날아가는 듯
군락을 이루어
화해를 하고
안부를 전하네

가는 잎과 부드러운 줄기
청초한 꽃송이가
은은하고 향긋하여

우리의 눈을 즐겁게 하고
기분을 좋게 한다.

Peacock Flower

Everywhere
In a good mood all the time
To live

In each gesture
On a long stem
Little flowers
A dense bloom

As if a peacock were flying
Constituting a community
In reconciliation
Say hello to you

Thin leaves and soft stems
Innocent flowers
In a subtle, fragrant way

To entertain our eyes
Make you feel better.

천냥금꽃

천냥금꽃은
실내공기 정화식물로
성격이 좋아
관상용으로 인기 있고

초록 잎 사이로
보이는
작고 빨간 열매는
돈을 불려주고

사업이
번창하길 바라는 마음으로

천냥금꽃을 키운다

내일의 행복을 위하여.

Thousand Gold Flower

Thousand gold flower
Indoor air purification plant
Good personality
Popular for ornamental purposes

Through the green leaves
Visible
Small red fruits
Giving you money

Business
With the hope of prospering

Growing a thousand flower

For tomorrow's happiness.

일일초꽃의 겨울

세월이 흘러
늦가을 서리가 내릴 무렵

화단에 일일초꽃
시들어 버리니
내버려 둘 수가 없네

화분에 심어
집안으로 옮기니

앙상한 줄기에
달린 이파리 몇 개에
노란빛이 반짝반짝

애지중지 키우니
푸른 잎이 돋아나고
꽃도 피어
나를 반기네

겨우내
내 사랑을
독차지한 일일초꽃

그대를 사랑하리!

Winter of Daily Flower

As time goes by
By the time the frosts of late autumn

A daily flower in a flower bed
Withered
I can't leave it alone

Plant in pot
I moved to the house

In the thin stem
I've got a few run-down leaves
A yellow glow

You raise a flower
Blue leaves spring up
Flowering
You're welcome to me

Throughout the winter
My love
A lofty day flower

I will love you!

루엘리아꽃

봄에는 나물로
꽃망울이 귀엽고
우아하게 꽃이 피어 신비롭다

꽃이 볼수록 단아하고
청순함을 느끼게 되어 신비롭다

더위 가뭄에도 강하고
병충해도 이겨내니 신비롭다

자색의 꽃 빛으로
매력적이고 신비롭다

여름에서 가을 내내
꽃을 볼 수 있어 신비롭다

항산화 약재 식물로
재배되어 신비롭다

꽃이 지고
씨방이 익으면
딱!
소리를 내며
씨앗을 주위로 날려 보내니
신비롭다.

Ruelia Flower

In spring, in herbs
Flower petals are cute
It is mysterious with graceful flowers

The more flowers you see, the more sweet
It is mysterious to feel innocent

It's strong against heat droughts
It is mysterious to overcome the sickness

With purple flower
Be attractive and mysterious

From summer to autumn
It is mysterious to see flowers

As an antioxidant medicinal plant
Be cultivated and mysterious

The flower wither
When the ovary is ripe
Just!
With a sound
They send the seeds around
It's mysterious.

칸나꽃

칸나꽃 앞에 서면

키가 크고
얼굴이 예뻐 행복하다

당당하게 목을 곧추세워
승자의 환희에 찬
웃음이 있어 행복하다

패자의 회한에 찬
쓴웃음을 지을 수 있어 행복하다

우아하게 서 있는 모습을
보여줄 수 있어 행복하다

붉게 피어
미인이라고 치켜세우면
정열적인 몸짓이 있어 행복하다

꽃잎의 아름다운 곡선에
에로틱한 느낌을
줄 수 있어 행복하다

존경하는 마음을 담은
꽃다발을
드릴 수 있어 행복하다.

Canna Flower

In front of the canna flower

Tall and tall
Be happy with a pretty face

With a proud head up
In the joy of the winner
Be happy with laughter

In the remorse of the loser
I am happy to have a bitter laugh

A graceful standing figure
Be happy to show

Blooming red
You call her a beauty
I am happy to have a passionate gesture

In the beautiful curve of petal
The erotic feeling
Be happy to give

With respect
A bouquet
I'm happy to give you.

부들꽃

연못가에 보란 듯이
귀여운 이름
생긴 것도 재미있네

원통 모양의 꽃
고양이 꼬리 같아

압축된 솜은
바닥에 까는 자리
솜털 방석으로

열매는
부싯깃으로 쓰이고

야생의 핫도그
먹고 싶은 소시지
벌레가 알을 까는 벌레 밭

여름에는 꽃
가을에는 열매로

마치 자연의 순리에
순종하는 듯!

A Fluffy Flower

As if it were visible by the pond
A cute name
It's fun to look like it

Cylindrical flowers
It's like a cat tail

Compressed cotton
A flooring spot
Fluffy cushion

Fruit
In a flint

Wild hot dogs
Sausages you want to eat
A worm field

Flowers in summer
In the fall, with fruit

As if it were natural
Like you're obeying!

가우라꽃

길가에 핀
조그마한 꽃송이들

자세히 보면
참으로 예쁘다

바람에 흔들흔들
산야에 핀 야생화

멀리서 보면
나비가 팔랑이는 듯

여기저기
오래오래 꽃이 피어

아름다운 여인이
떠나간 이를 그리워하듯
춤을 추네!

Gaura Flower

Blooming on the side of street
Small flower buds

On a closer view
It's so pretty

A wave of wind
Wildflowers in the mountains

From a distance
Like a butterfly flapping

Here and there
Long-time flowers bloom

A beautiful woman
As if he missed the one who left
You're dancing!

부용화

성천의 부용이
청순하고 아름다워

보는 순간
숨이 멈출 듯

사람들의 눈에 띄었네

세월이 흐르며
덩달아 부용도
문필에 심취하여

재색을 겸비한
정숙한 여인으로

미인을 상징하는 꽃
부용화(芙蓉花)로

예쁘게 피었네!

Bouyong Flower

Buoyong of Seongcheon
Innocent and beautiful

Moment of view
Breathless

It was noticed by the people

Over the years
Bouyong, too
In the writing

Be beautiful and talented
As a virtuous woman

Flowers symbolizing beauty
As bouyong flower

It's pretty!

꽃과 바람과 詩

제4부

아로니아꽃 그대

언제나
그대는 태양처럼
그대 혼자일 뿐

물레나물 꽃

산기슭 청정지역에
샛노란 물레나물꽃

임 그리워
바람에 흔들리는 모양이

물레 돌아가듯
노랑나비 날아와
날갯짓하고

들판에 그려지는 물레방아
가까이 보니
서로 바람개비 되어
바람 소리 내며 돌아가네

아, 그리워라
임을 향한 일편단심
추억에 드리운 물레방아!

Spinning Wheel Flower

In the clean area of the mountain
A yellow spinning wheel flower

I miss you
The shape of the wind

Like a spinning wheel
Yellow butterfly fly
I flapped my wings

A water mill drawn in a field
I can see close
Each other, it becomes pinwheel
You're going around with the wind

Oh, miss me
I'm determined to be Lim
The water mill in memory!

고삼꽃

한여름 무더위에
산들바람 살랑살랑

먹구름 사이로
주홍빛이 감도는 노란색
고삼 꽃봉오리

도레미파솔라시
음계 맞춰
이리저리 흔들며
노래 부르고

송알송알
고삼(苦蔘) 뿌리 찾는 소리
들리는 듯

인삼처럼 좋은 효능
감춰진 쓴맛을
그리워하는 그대에게

도둑놈의 지팡이가
발걸음을 멈추게 하네!

Sophora Root Flower

In the midsummer heat
Soft breeze

In the dark clouds
A yellow with scarlet color
Flower bud of sophora root

Doremipasolasi
Get the notes right
Waving around
Singing

Songal songal
The sound of find the root of old ginseng
As if it were audible

Good efficacy like ginseng
The hidden bitterness
To you whom I miss

The thief's staff
You are stopping me!

산해박꽃

나그네가
산해박에 묻는다

이름이 신기하네
네, 그렇습니다

어디에 사는가?
햇빛이 드는 풀밭에요

왜 산해박인가?
산에서 자라니까요

언제 일하나?
이른 아침이나 비가 올 때
활짝 웃는 모습을 보여줍니다

그대가 약재의 왕이라면서?
네, 그렇습니다
특히 신경쇠약과 불면증
치료쯤은

어떻게 종족을 늘리느냐?
털 씨앗으로 멀리 여행을 보냅니다

하지만
떠나간 벗들이 그립습니다.

Mountain Sea Flower

A traveler
Ask in mountain sea bream

I'm surprised by your name
Yes, sir

Where do you live?
It's a sunny grass

Why the mountain sea?
They grow up in the mountains

When do you work?
Early morning or when it rains
It shows a wide smile

You're the king of drug?

Yes, sir

Neurodebilitation and Insomnia

When it comes to treatment

How do you increase your race?

Travel far with fur seeds

But

I miss my friends who left.

물봉선꽃

물봉선 씨앗이
스스로 폭발해
물로 뛰어들어

봉선화를 닮고
물가에서 자라
가녀린 물봉선

오밀조밀
예쁜 모양새

고독을 즐기려
혼자 있고 싶을 때

물봉선꽃을 메시지로 보내면
어떨까?

물봉선의 당돌한 선언

'나를 건드리지 마!'

Impatiens Textori Flower

The seed of impatiens textori
It explodes itself
Dive into the water

It looks like impatiens
Grow up by the water
A thin impatiens textori

Delicately
A pretty shape

To enjoy solitude
When you want to be alone

I'll send a message to you
What do you think?

A grand declaration of impatiens textori

'Don't touch me!'

솔나물꽃

사각형 긴 줄기에
샛노란 꽃을 피운
아름다운 꽃

가뭄을 이기고
무리 지어
산들바람에 살랑살랑

드넓은 산야에
내리쬐는 햇빛으로
눈이 부신 솔나물꽃

돌연사를 막아주는
최고의 약재로

인간에게
고귀한 사랑을 받고

그대의 향기로
잊을 수 없는 추억을!

Bedstraw Flower

Square long stem
Blooming bright yellow flower
A beautiful flower

Overcame drought
In a group
Soft breeze

In a vast mountainous area
With the sunlight
Bright Bedstraw Flower

Abruptly blocking
With the best medicine

To man
In the noble love

By your scent
Unforgettable memories!

타래난초꽃

햇빛이 쨍쨍
내리쬐는 산야

가늘고 작아
풀 속에서는
잘 보이지 않는 타래난초

스스로
돋보이려

하늘로 올라가고 싶은 소녀

층층이
계단 만들어

그 꿈 이루려
밤낮으로
하늘 향해
꿈틀댄다네!

Tare Orchid Flower

The sun is shining
The mountain that shines down

Thin and small
In the grass
A poorly visible tare orchid

By oneself
Flattering

A girl who wants to go up into the sky

Stratified
Make a staircase

To achieve that dream
Day and night
For the sky
I'm wriggling!

크로커스꽃

한겨울을 지나
눈 속에서
솟아오르는 하얀 꽃송이

잎사귀보다 먼저
꽃으로 활짝 피었다가

밤이 되면
수줍은 듯
꽃 모양이 오므라든다

화사한 꽃 모양이 귀엽고
나중에 피는 이파리도
조화로워

환희와 기쁨으로
예쁘게 핀 크로커스꽃

보는 순간마다
후회 없는 사랑으로
미소가 가득.

Crocus Flower

Past the winter
In the snow
White flowers rising

Before the leaves
Blooming with flowers

At night
Shyly
The flower shape curls

The bright flower is cute
Even the leaves that bloom later on
In harmony

With joy and joy
A pretty crocus flower

Every moment you see
With love without regret
Full of smiles.

고독힌 솔체꽃

프릴 치마처럼
겹겹이 쌓여있는 꽃잎 속에
가득한 그대의 슬픔

금세 터질 듯한 꽃봉오리
새롭게 돋아나
그대의 외로움에
붉은빛이 감도네

깊은 산속을
쓸쓸히 헤매며

이루어질 수 없는 사랑을
가슴에 담고

사랑한다 말도 못 하고

슬픔과 외로움에
애틋한 미소만 짓네!

Solitary Scabiosa Flower

Like a frill skirt
In the petal in which the layer is piled up
The fullest sorrow of yours

A bursting bud
A new rise
In your loneliness
It's red

Deep in the mountains
Wandering forlornly

Love that can not be achieved
In the chest

I can't say I love you

In grief and loneliness
You just smile a little!

샐비어꽃

여름 화단의 왕

불타오르는 듯한 꽃송이에
향기 가득한 깨꽃이
활짝 피었다

한번 피더니
계속 피어서

마을 밖 길거리가
온통 화사해졌다

예쁘게
오래 피는 꿀 꽃

해마다
몇 포기씩 심은
추억의 꽃

불타는 내 마음을
아는지

내년에는 마당에도
심어봐야지

동네 꽃밭에도!

Salvia Flower

King of summer flower bed

In a burning flower bud
Sesame flowers full of scent
Be blooming

It bloom once
In constant bloom

The streets outside the village
It was all bright

Prettily
Honey flower that blooms for a long time

Year by year
I planted a few heads each
A flower of memories

My burning heart
Do you know

Next year, in the yard
I'll plant it

In the neighborhood flower garden!

아로니아꽃 그대

언제나
그대는 태양처럼
그대 혼자일 뿐

지금
우리에게는

불로장생
영원한 사랑
만병통치약
신이 내린 열매

이 모두가 남의 이야기
진실로
잘 기억하고 있다고 해도

세월이 흐르고 흘러
과거에도 미래에도
진정 내 것으로
만들 수 없는 그대

건강을 찾아
삶을 헤매다가
놓치고 마는 오늘

그리고….

Aronia Flower, You

Always
You are like the sun
You're alone

Now
For us

Perpetual youth
Eternal love
Panacea
A fruit of god

All of these are other people's stories
Truely
Even if you remember it well

As time goes by
In the past and in the future
Calm down with mine
I can't make you

Find health
Wandering through life
I'm missing today

And….

뚱딴지꽃

어느 사이 초가을
뚱딴지 꽃송이
멀리서 보아도
눈길을 사로잡는다

주위에
밤송이 올망졸망
탐스럽게 익어가고

아래로는
들국화 보란 듯이
사방에 피어 있네

울타리엔
늘 푸른 사철나무
온갖 작물을 에워싸고

아직은
단풍이 들지 않은 농장

당뇨병에 좋다 하여
돼지감자 굵은 뿌리를
캐서
바구니에 담는다.

Fatty Flower

In the early autumn
Fatty flowers
Even from a distance
Catch one's eye

Around
Chestnut in clusters
It's ripening up nicely

Down
As if it were a wild chrysanthemum
There's a bloom everywhere

In the fence
Always blue spindle tree
Encircling all kinds of crops

Not yet
A farm without a maple

It's good for diabetes
The thick roots of pork potatoes
Dig out
Put it in a basket.

꽃과 바람과 詩

제5부

포인세티아꽃

과거의 흔적이 된
겨울의 꽃
곱고 아름다운 축하의 꽃

수선화

따뜻한 봄날
지방의 조그마한 시골 마을
학교에 가고 올 때

정원마다
군락을 이루고
집집이 꽃밭에
예쁘게 피어 있는 수선화

가끔 지나면서
꽃을 만지고
향기를 맡으며
입맞춤하고
꺾어 오기도 한다

다시 세월을
돌이켜보니

아마
그게
시를 쓰는
계기가 되었나 보다.

Daffodil Flower

A warm spring day
A small rural village in the province
When you go to school and come back

In every garden
Forming a colony
The house is in the flower garden
A beautifully bloomed daffodil

As time passes by
Touch the flowers
Smelling
Kissing
Sometimes, I break it down

Time goes by again
Looking back

Maybe
Well
Writing poetry
Maybe it's a chance.

자두나무꽃

우리는 과수원에 세 들어 산다

자두나무 오얏나무 자도나무
이렇게 세쌍둥이는 순백(純白)의 꽃으로
호흡을 맞춰

4월에
아름다운 봄꽃으로 밀린 월세를 낸다

한여름 무더위에 땀을 뻘뻘
8월에는
빨갛게 익은 탐스러운 열매로
밀린 월세를 낸다

자두나무는
제날짜에 월세를 잘도 낸다.

Plum Tree Flower

We rent out the orchard

Plum tree, prunaria, jado tree
These triplets are pure white flowers
Work in harmony

In April
The rent is pushed by beautiful spring flowers

Sweaty in the heat of summer
In August
With the red ripe fruit
Pay a rent behind

Plum tree
Pay monthly rent well on the right date.

곰취꽃

숲속을 거닐다 보니
나무가 내게
말을 건네듯이

숲속의 풀벌레가
저마다
소리의 향연을 벌인다

시냇물에 발을 담그니
더위가 저 멀리 사라지고

향긋한 곰취꽃
곰이 좋아하는 곰취나물
먹어서 약이 되는 보물

맛과 향이 독특하여
산나물의 제왕
돼지고기 싸서 먹으면
맛이 있다는 여인의 슬기

산나물로 사랑받고
꽃으로도 귀여움받네!

Gomchi Flower

I walked through the woods
To me, the tree
As if to say

The grassworms in the woods
Each of them
Have a feast of sound

Soaking my feet in the stream
The heat is gone away

A fragrant gomchi flower
The gomchi herb that bear like
A treasure that is medicinally eaten

The taste and flavor are unique
King of wild plants
If you wrap it in pork and eat it
The wisdom of a woman of taste

Loved by wild plants
You're cute with flowers!

레몬나무꽃

레몬나무 한 그루를
뜰 앞에 심는다
귤 오렌지 한라봉보다 웃자라
어느 사이 키가 6m

계절이 바뀌며
꽃과 이파리가
별들과 노니더니

한바탕 찬 바람이 불어
꺾인 가지에
열매가 주렁주렁

레몬즙은 생선회에 뿌려 먹고
샐러드에 넣어 먹기도 하고
레몬청을 만들어
떡과 함께 찍어 먹고
레몬 잼은 빵에 발라 먹는다

상큼함을 더해주는
레몬꽃과 열매
아름답고 맛이 있다.

Lemon Tree Flower

A lemon tree
Plant in front of the courtyard
Grow more than tangerine orange hallabong
At some point, it is 6m tall

With the changing seasons
Flower and leaves
You played with the stars

A cold wind blew
On a broken branch
The fruit hang in clusters

Lemon juice is sprinkled with sashimi
I put it in a salad
Make lemon syrup
I'll eat with rice cake
Lemon jam is eaten on bread

It adds freshness
Lemon flowers and fruit
It's beautiful and delicious.

갈대꽃

그 척박한 땅에 뿌리 내려
대대로 제자리 지키는
습지의 갈대숲
한순간도 멈추지 않고
소르르 바람에 서걱거리네

철새 날아들고
노을을 그리워하는
긴 목 늘인 갈대의 순정이여

강물과 노래하며
바람에 시달려도
그리움에 사무치는 듯
블루스 춤을 춘다

인생도 갈대처럼
태생지 탓하지 않고
의연함을 보여 줄 수 있을까!

무심한 저 풍경 앞에
무엇이 그리운지
발길이 머물고
소슬한 바람은
너를 그렇게 또 울리는구나.

Reed Flower

It's rooted in the barren land
In place for generations
Wetland reed forest
Without a moment's pause
The wind crunchs gently

Migratory birds
Nostalgic
The sheer purity of long-necked reeds

Singing with the river
In the wind
As if it were a longing
Dance blues

Life is like a reed
Without blaming your birthplace
Can you show me your probableness?

In front of that indifferent landscape
What I miss
With a long way to go
The wind is sore
Making you cry again.

수박꽃의 일생

과일 가게에 들어서니
수박은 친근한데
수박꽃은 낯설다

무심코 뱉은 씨가
비바람에 땅에 묻혀
새싹을 틔운다

원두막에서 내려다본
한여름의 텃밭

잦은 비에 쑥쑥 자라
개화 한 달 만에
폭풍 성장으로
커다랗게 영글어가는 수박

큰마음을 가지지 않고서야
가능한 일인가?

The Life of Watermelon Flower

I went into the fruit shop
Watermelon is friendly
Watermelon flowers are unfamiliar

Seed it spat out casually
Put it under the ground in the rain and wind
Sprout

Looking down from the hut
A midsummer garden

Grow up in frequent rain
In a month of bloom
Storm-growingly
A large, lush watermelon

Without having a big heart
Is that possible?

감국꽃 향기

파란 물감이 떨어질 듯
눈이 부시도록 드리워진
가을 하늘 아래

감국꽃 꽃잎에 맺힌
영롱한 아침 이슬

저 멀리
산새 소리가 들리고

구름은
노란 감국꽃 위에 앉아
감국에 취해
가을을 노래하네

가을 산야는
불로장생을 돕고
재앙을 막아주는 감국꽃 천지

가을의 향기가
온종일
바람 타고 흐르네!

Chrysanthemum Flower Scent

Blue paints are falling
Dazzling
Under the autumn sky

Arboreal
A brilliant morning dew

Far away
I hear the sound of a mountain bird

Clouds
Sitting on a yellow chrysanthemum flower
Drunk in chrysanthemum
Sing autumn

The autumn mountains
To help the eternal life
The chrysanthemum flower to prevent disaster

The scent of autumn
All day
The wind is blowing!

아스타꽃

아스타꽃이 피는 마을에
가을이 다녀갔네

가을 여행지로
믿는 사람들끼리
신뢰하며
추억을 남기려
다녀갔네

꿀벌도
하얀 아스타 꽃향기 따라
빠지면 안 된다고
다녀갔네

팔랑거리는 아스타꽃 위로
고추잠자리 춤추며
다녀갔네

힐링이 되는 가을 여행
아스타꽃이 핀
길을 따라
그대와 걷고 싶네!

Asta Flower

In the village where asta flowers bloom
Autumn is gone

Fall travel destination
Among people who believe
Trust
To make memories
I went

Honeybees, too
Following the scent of white asta flowers
I can't miss it
I went

Above the fluttering asta flowers
Red dragonfly dancing
I went

A healing autumn trip
Asta flower bloomed
Along the way
I want to walk with you!

흰독말풀꽃

흰독말풀꽃은
예쁘지만, 거리를 두고 바라본다

흰독말풀꽃은
아름답지만, 악마의 나팔이다

흰독말풀꽃은
성질은 따뜻하고 독성이 강하다

흰독말풀꽃은
만지면 안 되는 꽃
반려견은 멀리 둔다

흰독말풀꽃은
미량으로 독이 되고 약이 된다

흰독말풀꽃은
밤새도록 향기를 품다가
낮에는 사라진다

흰독말풀꽃을 좋아하는 것은
덧없는 사랑
강한 독성으로 환각을 일으킨다.

White Poison Ivy Flower

The white poison ivy flower
It's pretty, but I look away

The white poison ivy flower
It's beautiful, but it's a devil's trumpet

The white poison ivy flower
It is warm and toxic

The white poison ivy flower
A flower that should not be touched
keep the dog away

The white poison ivy flower
It becomes poisoned and drugged in trace amounts

The white poison ivy flower
I've been smelling all night
It disappears during the day

The love of the white poison ivy flower
A fleeting love
The Strong toxicity causes hallucinations.

포인세티아꽃

그곳에 가면
내 정신을 빼앗아버리는
화원이 있다

예쁘게 다듬어진 꽃들
시들어 못생긴 꽃들
잔잔하게 미소짓는 꽃들
두 팔 벌려 환영하는 꽃들
스스로 안기어 노래 부르는 꽃들

겨울의 문턱에 닿아
비바람에 씻기고
삶에 할퀴어

과거의 흔적이 된
겨울의 꽃
곱고 아름다운 축하의 꽃
포인세티아

진한 초록색과 붉은색으로
겨울을 따뜻하게 하네

집집이 겨울 시즌에
자주 보이는 꽃

연말이면 생각나는
크리스마스의 꽃

'축하합니다.'

Poinsettia Flower

If you go there
It takes my mind away
There's a flower garden

Beautifully trimmed flowers
Withered and ugly flowers
Flowers that smile calmly
Flowers welcomed with open arms
Flowers that hug themselves and sing

At the threshold of winter
Wash up in the rain and wind
Scratch one's life

A trace of the past
Winter flowers
A pretty and beautiful flower of celebration
Poinsettia

In dark green and red
Warming the winter

In the winter season
Flowers that you see often

At the end of the year
Christmas flowers

'Congratulations.'

무을녀꽃

가는 겨울이 아쉬운 듯
무을녀 꽃망울을
집집이
정원마다 흩어 뿌린다

꽃망울이 조심조심
부풀어 오른다

잎은 작고 통통하며
가는 줄기에
촘촘하게 박혀 있어
꽃다발 같은 무을녀화(舞乙女花)

고목에 꽃이 핀 듯
신기하네

수형(樹形)이 아름다워
늘어지는 줄기가
춤추는 듯
부드러운 곡선

가까이 보면
더욱더 그리운
하얀 꽃 빛의 아픔
활활 타올라
사랑의 열병 앓는다.

A Radish Girl Flower

The winter is a pity
Radish girl flowers
Door to door
Spread out in every garden

Watch out for the buds
Swell up

The leaves are small and plump
On the thin stem
It's tightly embedded
A radish girl flowers like a bouquet

As if flowers had bloomed in the old tree
That's amazing

The shape of a tree is beautiful
A drooping stem
Dancingly
Smooth curve

At close range
Even more nostalgic
The pain of white flower
A lively burn
I have a fever of love.

꽃과 바람과 詩

초판인쇄 2022년 1월 24일 초판발행 2022년 1월 29일

지은이   장현경
펴낸이   장현경 펴낸곳   엘리트출판사
등록일   2013년 2월 22일 제2013-10호

서울특별시 광진구 긴고랑로15길 11 (중곡동)
전화 010-5338-7925
E-mail : wedgus@hanmail.net

정가 12,000원

ISBN 979-11-87573-33-3 03810